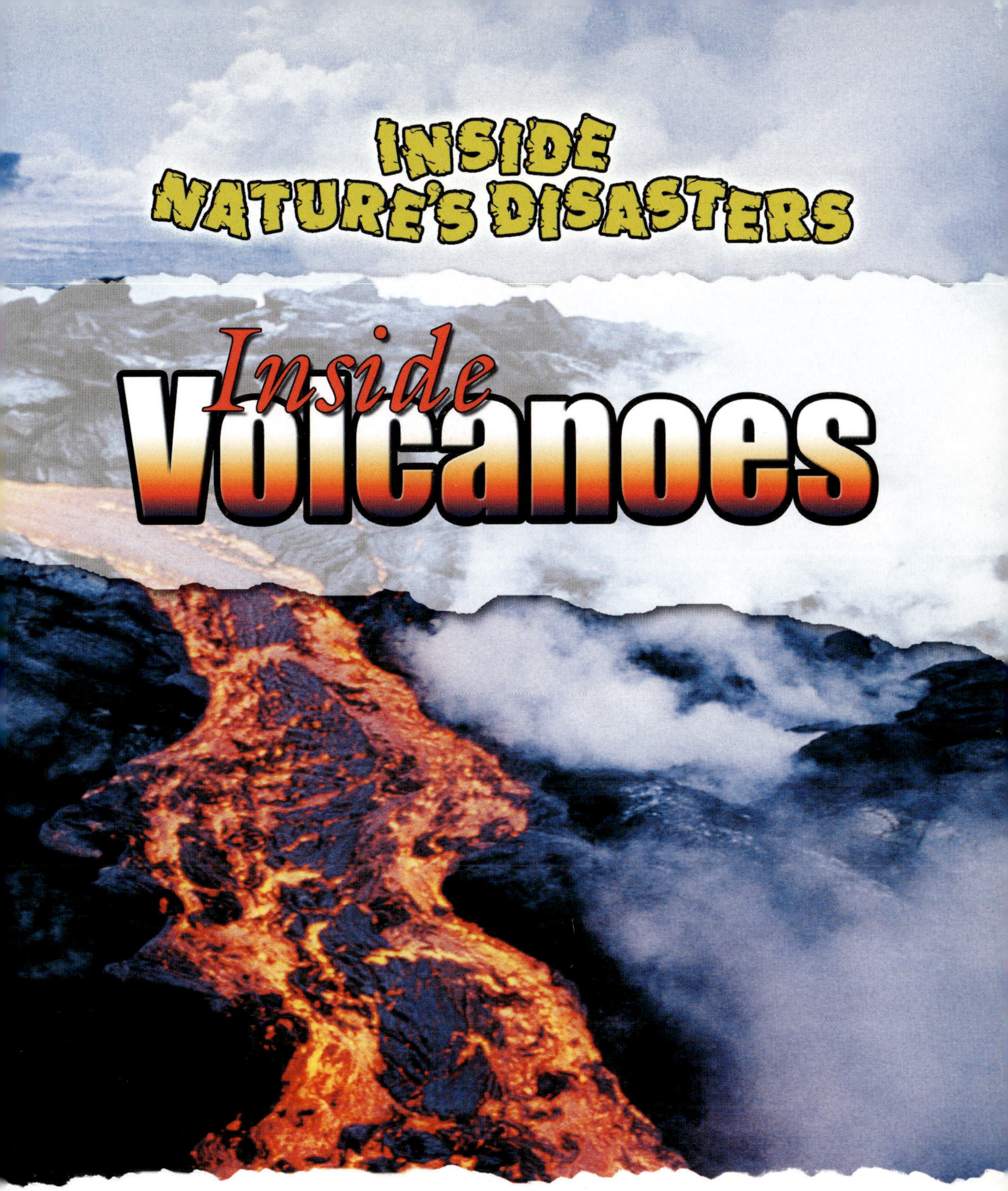

INSIDE NATURE'S DISASTERS

Inside Volcanoes

Philip Steele

GARETH**STEVENS**
GS
PUBLISHING
A Member of the WRC Media Family of Companies

Please visit our web site at: www.garethstevens.com
For a free color catalog describing Gareth Stevens Publishing's
list of high-quality books and multimedia programs,
call 1-800-542-2595 or 1-800-387-3178 (Canada).
Gareth Stevens Publishing's fax: (414) 332-3567.

Library of Congress Cataloging-in-Publication Data

Steele, Philip, 1948-
　　Inside volcanoes / by Philip Steele.
　　　　p. cm. — (Inside nature's disasters)
　　Includes bibliographical references and index.
　　ISBN-10: 0-8368-7250-9 — ISBN-13: 978-0-8368-7250-7 (lib. bdg.)
　　1. Volcanoes—Juvenile literature.　I. Title.　II. Series.
　　QE521.3.S734　2007
　　551.21—dc22　　　　　　　　　　　　　　　　2006009694

This North American edition first published in 2007 by
Gareth Stevens Publishing
A Member of the WRC Media Family of Companies
330 West Olive Street, Suite 100
Milwaukee, WI 53212 USA

This revised and updated U.S. edition copyright © 2007 by Gareth Stevens, Inc.

Original edition copyright © 2002 by ticktock Entertainment Ltd. First published in Great Britain
in 1999 by ticktock Publishing Ltd., Unit 2, Orchard Business Centre, North Farm Road,
Tunbridge Wells, Kent, TN2 3XF.

Gareth Stevens editor: Richard Hantula
Gareth Stevens cover design: Dave Kowalski
Gareth Stevens managing editor: Mark Sachner
Gareth Stevens art direction: Tammy West

Picture Credits: t = top, b = bottom, c = center, l = left, r= right,
OFC = outside front cover, OBC = outside back cover, IFC = inside front cover
AKG; 2c & 2br. Ancient Art & Architecture; 29cr, 29tr. Ann Ronan/Image Select; 13br.
Anthony Blake Photo Library; 28br. The British Museum; 2tl. CFCL/Image Select; 5bl. Giraudon;
2bl, 3br, 5cr. Images; 11cr, 25tr. Mary Evans; 5tr. NASA; 4tl. Oxford Scientific Films; OFC. Pix;
4b, 8tl, 10br, 21br, 21bl, 24tl. Planet Earth; OFC (inset), OBC (top), IFC, 7cr, 8c, 12c, 14/15b,
14b, 17tr, 18/19t, 20tr, 20bl, 23br, 26cr, 28/29 (main pic) & 32. Rex; 6b, 13cr, 14t, 16/17 (main
pic), 17bl, 17br, 19cb, 18tl, 18bl, 18br, 18bl, 23c, 25cl, 28tl. Science Photo Library; 4/5t, 6cl, 6t,
9tr, 9c, 10/11 (main pic), 12/13 (main pic), 12tl, 21tr, 23tr, 26bl & OBC, 27br, 28cl, 30/31t, 30cb,
30cl, 31br, 31bl. Still Pictures; 20br, 20/21t. The Stock Market; 2/3t. Telegraph Colour Library;
6/7t, 7br, 15c. Tony Stone; 12b, 14cr, 22/23 (main pic), 24b, 24/25t, 26/27 (main pic).

Every effort has been made to trace the copyright holders for the photos used in this book. The
publisher apologizes, in advance, for any unintentional omissions and would be pleased to insert
the appropriate acknowledgements in any subsequent edition of this publication.

Printed in the United States of America

1 2 3 4 5 6 7 8 9 10 09 08 07 06

CONTENTS

A scientist stands like a knight at the gates of hell (below). His armor is a silver, flameproof suit. Behind him rises a terrifying wall of red-hot, molten rock. It has burst from the depths of the Earth.

THE GATES OF HELL

The ground begins to shake and rumble. Mountain peaks are blasted apart. The sky turns dark, and lightning forks and flashes. The air becomes poisonous, stinking, choking. Long ago, terrified human beings believed that volcanoes were the work of angry gods or goddesses, of giants or evil spirits. Some said that volcanoes were gateways to hell. Sometimes human sacrifices were thrown into the crater, to appease the gods. It was not until the 1900s that scientists such as Alfred Wegener (1880–1930) began to understand the structure of the Earth's thin outer layer, or crust. Scientists are still learning the truth about volcanoes today — and it really is stranger than fiction.

In Hawaii, there is an ancient custom of making offerings of berries to Pele (above), the Polynesian volcano goddess. Pele is also known as Hina-Ai-Malama, "she who eats the Moon."

GREEK FIRE

Some ancient thinkers tried to figure out what caused volcanoes if they weren't the work of gods. The Greek philosopher Aristotle (*left*; 384-322 B.C.) believed that the Earth was honeycombed with caverns, which sucked in the winds. These were heated by great fires and then belched out again, creating volcanoes.

THE DEVIL'S DOMINION

Many Christians have thought of hell as an underground realm of darkness, fire, and glowing embers. The devil himself was said to smell of "brimstone" (sulfur). Ideas like these probably had their origins in people's experience of volcanoes and craters such as Mount Etna in Sicily. Volcanoes were unknown, terrifying, and deadly forces — surely, the work of the devil.

This nightmarish vision of hell and its torments (left and above) was painted by the Dutch artist Hieronymus Bosch, who lived from around 1450 to 1516.

VULCAN'S WORKSHOP

Our word "volcano" comes from the name Vulcan, or Vulcanus.
From at least 1500 B.C. until about A.D. 400, the ancient Greeks
worshipped a fire god called Hephaestus. The Romans worshipped the
same god, and called him Vulcanus. The god was said to own great
furnaces, where metals were melted and forged. These were located
inside Mount Etna on the island of Sicily. Etna (*above*) still sparks like
a blacksmith's forge today.

*According to one legend, Hephaestus hammered out a magic
shield for the Greek hero Achilles (above). The shield depicted
the world and everything that was in it.*

KRAKATOA, 1883

The volcanic island of Krakatoa near Java in Indonesia erupted in late August 1883 (*right*). The sound of the explosions could be heard over 10 percent of the Earth's surface. At least 36,000 people were killed.

This picture (above) taken from space shows a round hole on Sumbawa island in Indonesia. This hole is a caldera, or huge crater, about 4 miles (6 kilometers) wide, that was formed when Mount Tambora erupted and collapsed in 1815.

VESUVIUS, A.D. 79

DEATH OF A ROMAN ADMIRAL

In A.D. 104 a Roman writer called Pliny the Younger wrote to the historian Tacitus to describe how his uncle, Pliny the Elder (an admiral and man of letters), had died in A.D. 79. Pliny the Elder, then age 56, was stationed with the Roman fleet at Misenum. After lunch on August 24, his sister Plinia pointed out a large cloud rising above the mountains. Pliny hurried to the harbor and ordered the fleet to be launched. He wanted to carry out a rescue mission and, as a scientist, take detailed notes of everything he saw. As he approached the danger zone, ash and stones were raining down from Mount Vesuvius. Going ashore at a friend's house at Stabiae, Pliny ate and rested. However, soon Vesuvius was going full blast, and thick, choking ash was everywhere. Pliny suffocated on the shore, where his body was found two days later.

AN ANCIENT CRATER

These cliffs (*left*) on the Greek island of Thíra, or Santorini, are crater walls, formed by one of the most massive volcanic eruptions ever experienced. Around 1500 B.C., much of the island was blasted into oblivion. Clouds of ash and gas drifted over the island of Crete, 70 miles (110 km) away. Thíra erupted again in 1926.

MOUNTAINS OF DOOM

A volcano is an opening in the Earth's crust. Streams of molten rock called lava erupt, or burst out, from the opening. Ashes and rocks may be hurled into the sky. As the lava cools, it hardens and forms new rock. Lava and ash may pile up into a cone, which soon grows into a mountain. Some volcanoes are very violent. Others are more peaceful. Some volcanoes erupt almost all the time, while others erupt only every few hundred or thousand years. Volcanoes that are erupting now or are expected to erupt in the future are said to be active. Those that were exhausted long ago are called extinct. It is all too easy to write off a volcano as extinct — as scientists have found to their cost.

Only two people out of some 30,000 living in St. Pierre, on the Caribbean island of Martinique, survived the catastrophic eruption (above) of Mount Pelée on May 8, 1902.

Excavations by archaeologists have uncovered Bronze Age towns on Thíra. Shown here (left) is Akrotíri, where fine buildings decorated with beautiful paintings were destroyed by the eruption that occurred around 1500 B.C.

VESUVIUS THE DESTROYER

Mount Vesuvius rises 4,200 feet (1,280 meters) above the Bay of Naples in southern Italy. The height and shape of this volcano has changed many times in history, as the peak has been repeatedly shattered by eruptions and then built up again. The most famous eruption was in A.D. 79, when the towns of Pompeii, Oplontis, Stabiae, and Herculaneum were all destroyed. Vesuvius is a serial killer. Eruptions in the past few centuries included a major one in 1631, as well as eruptions in 1779, 1794, 1822, 1872, 1906, 1929, and — most recently — in 1944. This painting (*above*) shows an 18th-century eruption.

FROM THE DEPTHS

To understand how volcanoes work, we need to take an imaginary journey to the center of our planet. Its central region, or core, is a ball made up mainly of iron and nickel. The inner part of the core is solid, but the core's outer layer is molten. The distance from Earth's center to the top of the core is about 2,160 miles (3,480 km). Above the core lies about 1,800 miles (2,900 km) of mantle, made of various materials, including metals. The lower part of this layer is rather rigid, although the rock is hot enough to flow slowly. The upper mantle is relatively soft and has pockets of hot, molten rock. The Earth's top layer, the crust, averages about 25 miles (40 km) thick beneath the continents, but just 4 miles (7 km) thick beneath the oceans. The crust is constantly being created and shaped by restless forces deep inside the planet.

THE ROCK FACTORY

We often think of our planet as solid and unchanging. In fact it has been developing ever since it was formed about 4.6 billion years ago. The inside of the Earth (*above*) acts as a giant power plant. The red areas in the mantle (colored yellow here) show rising hot, molten rock, which forms new surface rock. Old surface rock (blue) sinks and is melted down.

Earth's core

CENTRAL HEATING

At the Earth's core the pressure is awesome, and the temperature can be as high as 10,800 °Fahrenheit (6,000 °Celsius) or more. This causes molten rock, or magma, to rise through the mantle toward the crust. These magma flows driven by heat are called convection currents. Magma that bursts through the crust is the building material for new oceanic and continental crust.

This computer image (left) shows the movements of the convection currents around the core. The colors show variations in temperature. Dark blue is the coolest at 577 °F (303 °C). Red is the hottest at 2,190 °F (1,200 °C).

An abandoned truck is engulfed by a great flood of lava (right) after an eruption in Hawaii. The forces that shape the Earth's crust are both violent and unstoppable. They are necessary for the survival of the planet but can spell disaster for the people who live on its surface.

RIVERS OF FIRE

Once magma has burst out into the air or sea, it is called lava. Here (*left*), red-hot lava forms a long, glowing river on Mauna Loa, Hawaii. As it flows, the molten rock slows, cools, and hardens to form new rock.

KILAUEA, HAWAII, 1990

A smoldering stream of lava from Kilauea Crater, in the southern part of the island of Hawaii, inches its way into town. Lava can erupt at temperatures of up to 2,200 °F (1,200 °C). Even as it cools, it is still more than hot enough to set buildings afire and melt roads.

Weak spots in the Earth's crust crack open under the force of the magma welling up from below. Sometimes lava oozes out quietly, sometimes it is spewed up with extreme violence. Here (right), lava from a volcano in the Hawaiian islands spouts and splutters like boiling, red-hot jam.

RING OF FIRE

We often say that something is as solid as rock. In reality, while the outermost layer of the Earth is rigid, it is also cracked, like a fragile eggshell. The cracked sections, called tectonic plates, are supported by the oozing, soft rocks of the mantle. The unstable borders between the plates are danger zones for both earthquakes and volcanoes. The convection currents in the mantle make the plates move, but very slowly. Over the ages, these currents have caused the continents to change positions. Where plates move apart beneath an ocean, a rift forms in the ocean floor. Magma wells up to form new crust, creating a ridge of underwater mountains on either side of the crack.

Smoke pours through vents called fumaroles (above) in Hawaii Volcanoes National Park. The Hawaiian Islands were formed by volcanoes that developed not at the border between tectonic plates, but at a "hot spot" in the Earth's crust. Hot spots mark areas of great activity in the mantle, where magma punches its way through a plate.

Lava flows create new rock to fill the gap formed where plates move apart. The lava heats up the water. "Chimneys" of minerals build up at cracks called vents, spouting out gases (left) that bubble up through the water.

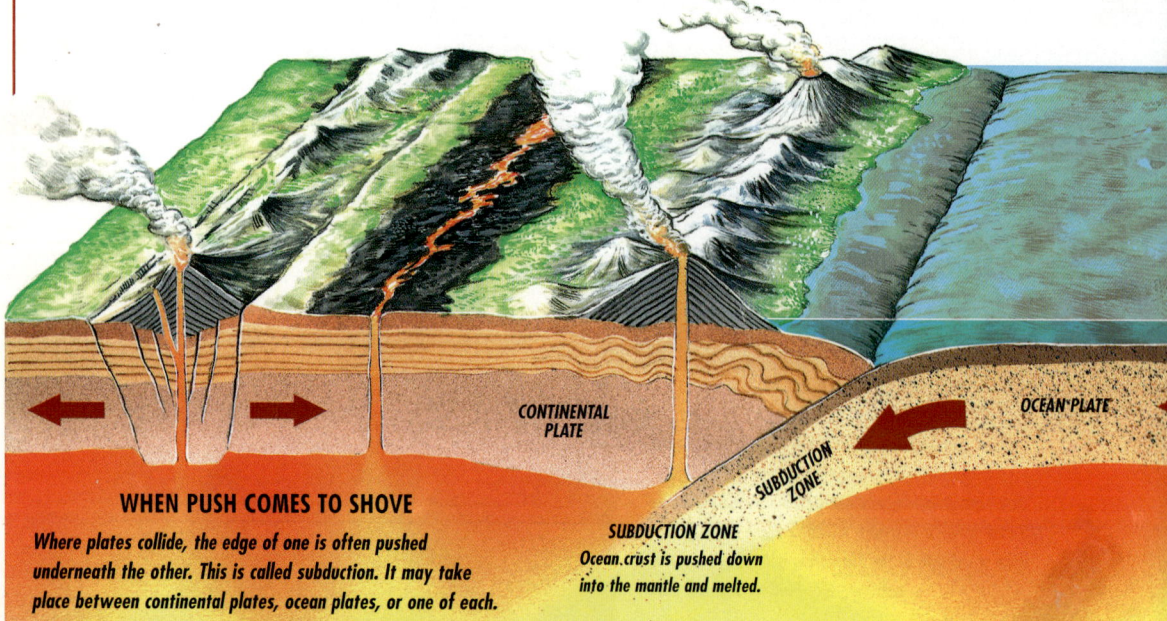

CONTINENTAL PLATE

OCEAN PLATE

SUBDUCTION ZONE

WHEN PUSH COMES TO SHOVE
Where plates collide, the edge of one is often pushed underneath the other. This is called subduction. It may take place between continental plates, ocean plates, or one of each.

SUBDUCTION ZONE
Ocean crust is pushed down into the mantle and melted.

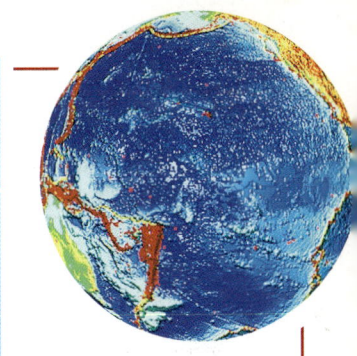

RING OF FIRE

Many volcanoes and earthquakes are located at plate boundaries along the rim of the Pacific Ocean. This "Ring of Fire" (above) extends from the Andes Mountains up to Alaska then over to Japan and down to New Zealand.

THE WORLD'S PLATES

The plates that make up the Earth's rigid outer layer are constantly moving, at a speed of just an inch or two (a few centimeters) a year. This small movement sets off earthquakes and volcanic eruptions, as well as creating mountain ranges and deep-sea trenches. The lines on the map (*above*) show the edges of the chief plates. It is at such boundaries that most earthquakes occur.

Volcanic activity beneath the ocean floor off the coast of Iceland created a new island called Surtsey between 1963 and 1967 (left). The new island was named after Surtur, lord of the land of fire giants in ancient Norse mythology.

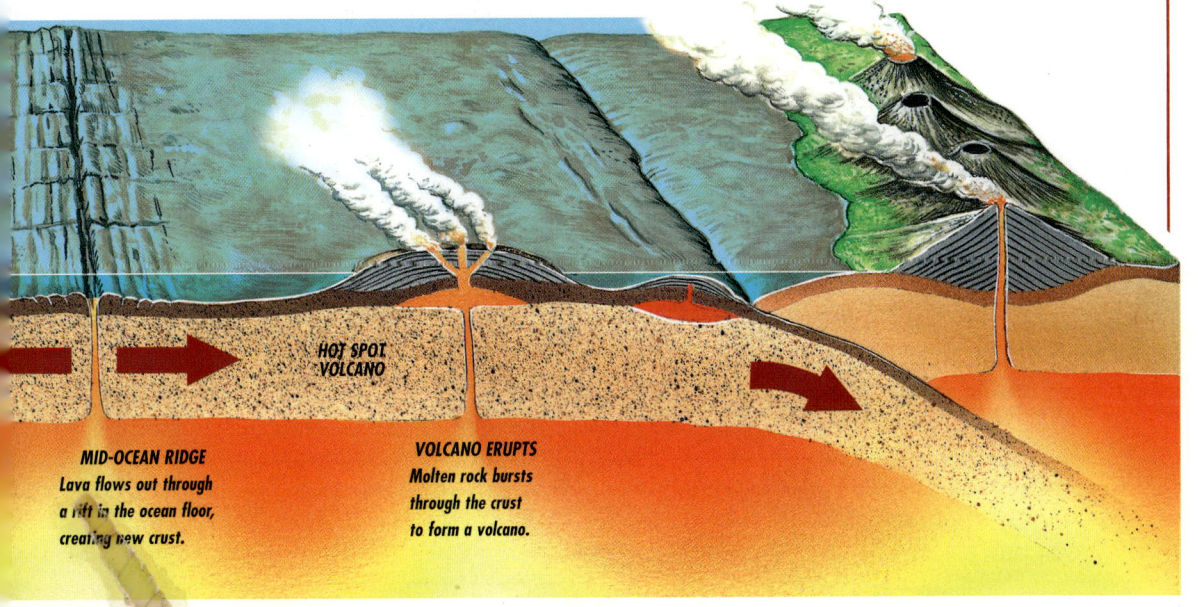

MID-OCEAN RIDGE
Lava flows out through a rift in the ocean floor, creating new crust.

VOLCANO ERUPTS
Molten rock bursts through the crust to form a volcano.

VESUVIUS, 1631

DEATH IN DECEMBER

Early in the morning of December 16, 1631, the peasants of the Italian region of Campania were herding their cattle and the priests were in their churches preparing for the festival of Christmas – when Vesuvius erupted again. There had already been months of earth tremors, and the crater was gradually filling with lava. At midday, however, fissures burst open unexpectedly on the southwestern slopes of the volcano. Hot lava flooded out in great rivers. Later there were torrential mudslides and new lava flows. Eyewitnesses reported massive falls of ash in the city of Naples. Thousands of people perished, many in the town of Resina, on the site of ancient Herculaneum.

Sometimes a small crack appears at the side or base of a volcano, leaking gas. Under massive pressure, it may tear open into a long fissure, as happened at Krafla in Iceland in 1977. Here (right) we see the 1.2-mile (2-km) fissure releasing large quantities of fluid lava.

ETNA UNPLUGGED

Mount Etna, on the Mediterrnean island of Sicily (left), sits on top of such a large amount of rising magma that it is almost constantly erupting. It rarely has time to build up a large solid plug. This means that the eruptions from its vent are less pressured and less violent than some others.

INSIDE THE VOLCANO

Red-hot magma from the Earth's upper mantle rises into large reservoirs or chambers inside the Earth's crust. Some of the magma seeps between layers of surface rock, resulting, when it cools, in a body of rock called a sill. Some of it may be trapped inside an old fissure, resulting in a body of rock called a dike.

Some magma bursts upward and escapes through volcano vents. Repeated eruptions of lava build up steep mountain sides around a central vent. Magma and gases under great pressure also force their way to the surface through secondary vents and fumaroles, which leak gases and steam. The inside of a volcano may be a honeycomb of pipes, vents, and fissures. After an eruption, the vents may be plugged as the magma cools and hardens.

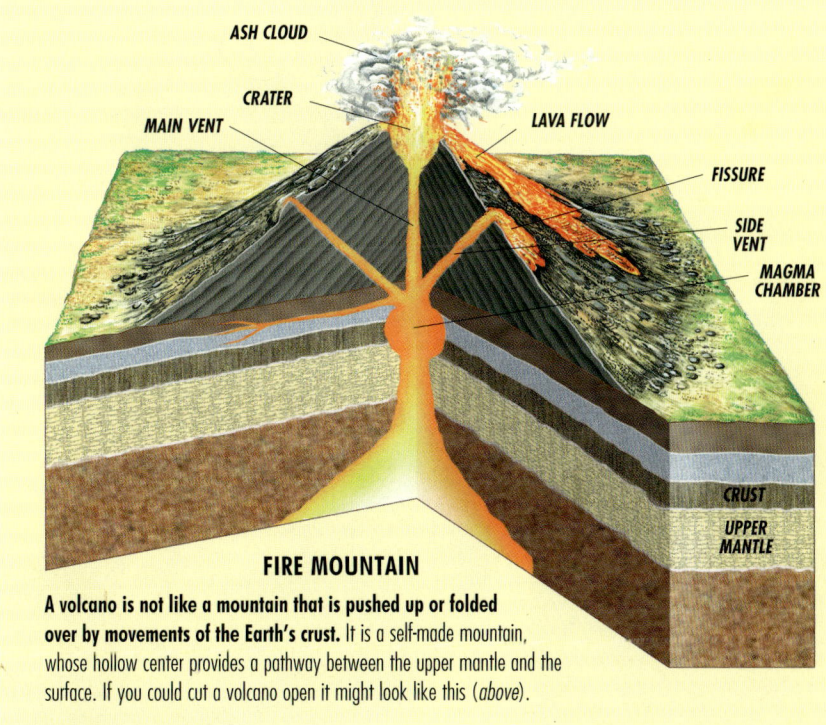

ASH CLOUD
CRATER
MAIN VENT
LAVA FLOW
FISSURE
SIDE VENT
MAGMA CHAMBER
CRUST
UPPER MANTLE

FIRE MOUNTAIN
A volcano is not like a mountain that is pushed up or folded over by movements of the Earth's crust. It is a self-made mountain, whose hollow center provides a pathway between the upper mantle and the surface. If you could cut a volcano open it might look like this (*above*).

THE HOLLOW TOOTH

When a violent volcanic eruption blasts the plug from a vent, it shatters the peak and leaves behind a crater. Some craters still connect with a vent to the magma chamber below, while others are blocked off by new plugs of lava and ash. Some of the most impressive craters are called calderas (*left*). These are formed when a massive blast empties the magma chamber, causing the volcano to collapse in on itself.

AN OMINOUS SILENCE

Like its neighbor, Mount Etna, the volcano forming the island of Stromboli is active most of the time. The mountain rumbles and grumbles. However, when it falls quiet, local residents expect trouble. The quiet often means rockfalls have blocked the vent and pressure is building up for a more violent eruption.

SIGNS AND WARNINGS

Volcanic activity is hard to predict. Even scientists who have been studying a volcano are sometimes taken by surprise. However there are warning signs, some of which have been recognized for thousands of years. There is often an increase in seismic activity (earthquakes and tremors) in the region of the volcano. More and more gases pour out of the crater or from side vents, fumaroles, and fissures.

They may stink of the mineral sulfur, which smells like rotten eggs. There may be rumbling and other strange noises as magma rises up inside the mountain. Sometimes the whole mountainside bulges from the force of magma, causing buildings to be lifted up and the sea to fall back from the shoreline.

SNAKE WATCH

Reports from many parts of the world suggest that the earth tremors and rising ground temperatures that precede an eruption drive snakes (left) out of their crevices and burrows.

MOUNT ST. HELENS, 1980

"I AM PART OF THE MOUNTAIN"

On April 30, 1980, the most dangerous area around Mount St. Helens in Washington State was declared a "Red Zone." Access to it was forbidden to everyone but scientists. Property owners in the zone were evacuated, but one 83-year-old man, named Harry Truman, refused to leave his house by Spirit Lake. On May 12 there was a large earthquake, but Harry and his 16 cats stayed put. "I am part of the mountain," he told the police patrol. Six days later the mountain collapsed. Harry perished as his home was buried beneath a cliff of ash and stone.

WHITE ISLAND, NEW ZEALAND

One measure of a volcano's activity is the plume of smoke rising from its summit. White Island (*above*), the peak of a submarine volcano in New Zealand's Bay of Plenty, offers other clues too. Mud boils and bubbles, and whistling jets of steam escape from the ground.

COUNTDOWN: MOUNT ST. HELENS

In the late 1960s, scientists warned that Mount St. Helens, a volcano in Washington State, should be carefully watched. From 1975 until 1980, no less than 44 small earthquakes were recorded around the peak. In early 1980 the earthquakes became massive and increasingly frequent. The crater grew, and long fissures opened up. The mountainside began to bulge outward. On May 18, 1980, Mount St. Helens erupted in a terrifying explosion (*below*). This infrared photo (*left*) was taken the day after.

RUN FOR YOUR LIFE!

People flee from the violent eruption of Vesuvius in 1906 (*above*). A scientific observatory had opened on the mountain in 1845. Before the volcano erupted, scientists reported tremors, choking gases, and a strange buzzing noise from inside the mountain.

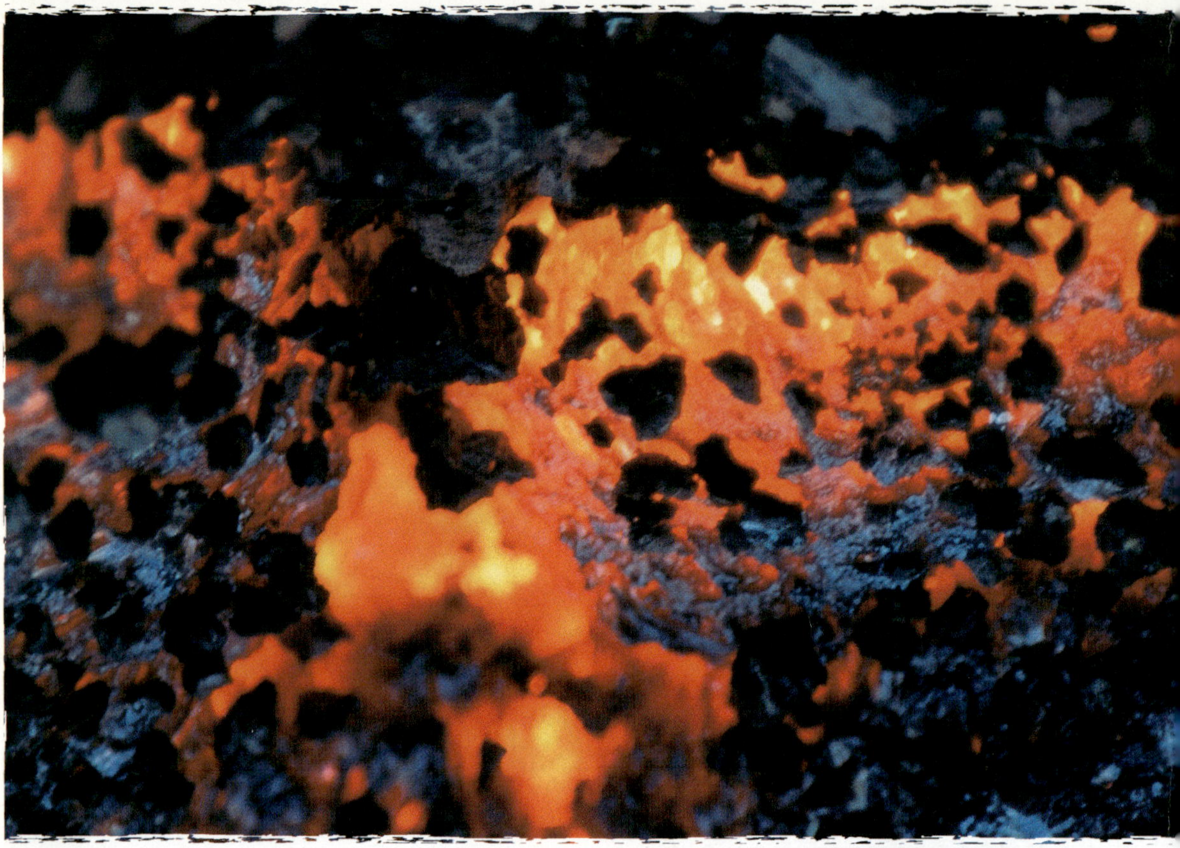

THE ROUGH STUFF

Lava rolls down the mountainside. This type of lava (*above*) is known by a Hawaiian name, *aa*. It is rough and contains sharp-edged blocks. It is cooler, slower, and stickier than other types of lava.

KRAKATOA, 1883

SAILING ON THE RIM OF HELL

On the night of August 26, 1883, a British sea captain, W. J. Watson of the Charles Bal, was sailing through the Sunda Strait between the islands of Sumatra and Java. As he passed the island of Krakatoa, piles of ash and hot stone showered down onto the wooden deck. The crew, fearing for their lives, shoveled the debris into the sea as fast as it fell. The air stank of sulfur, and the sailors could hardly breathe. Lightning forked through the sky, and the electrical glow known as "St. Elmo's Fire" flickered around the masts. The following morning there was an eerie silence for a time – then at 10:00 A.M., the whole island was blasted into the atmosphere with an ear-splitting roar.

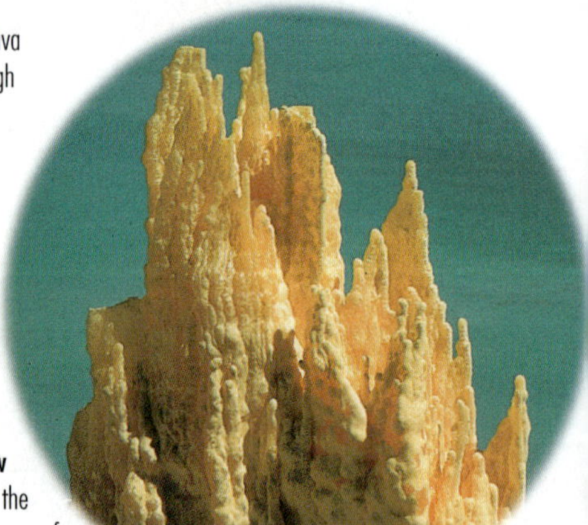

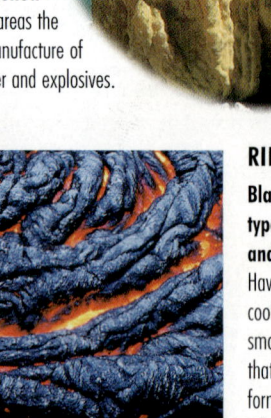

SOLID SULFUR

Volcanic gases contain high levels of sulfur, which solidifies as the gases cool and forms bright yellow crystals (*right*). In some volcanic areas the sulfur is mined for use in the manufacture of various products, including rubber and explosives.

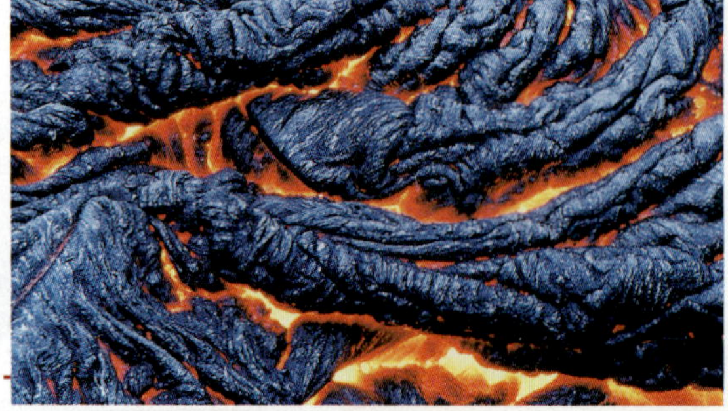

RIPPLES OF ROCK

Black and extremely hot, this type of lava flow (*left*) is fast and fluid. It is called by the Hawaiian word *pahoehoe*. As it cools, it turns into rock with a smooth, rippled surface. Lava that emerges under the sea forms rounded blocks called pillows.

BLOWING ITS TOP

A volcanic eruption can blow half a mountain apart. It is an awesome event. The deafening roar from the eruption of Krakatoa in 1883 could be heard on the island of Rodrigues, 3,000 miles (4,800 km) away on the other side of the Indian Ocean. A survivor of the Mount St. Helens eruption of 1980 said that it sounded as if the whole mountain had been placed in a giant concrete mixer. Various factors influence just how explosive an eruption will be.

Is the vent plugged by cooled magma or debris? If so, the pressure will be greater. Do the volcano's rocks contain water? If so, this can instantly turn into steam, expanding 200 times and smashing through solid rock.

A COLD PLUNGE

With Hawaiian volcanoes, lava eruptions from the caldera may tower up to 1,600 feet (500 m). Along fissures, lava may burst out in a long series of lower spouts. It may then start a journey of 20 miles (30 km) or more before cooling. Lava often flows into the sea (right), where it cools into cliffs of black rock.

Spectators watch in awe as lava pours from the volcanic Galapagos Islands into the Pacific Ocean (left). Clouds of steam rise from the cold ocean water.

MOUNT PELÉE, 1902

BAD ANCHORAGE

On the morning of May 8, 1902, the Roraima, a steamship owned by the Quebec Line, was anchored off the port of St. Pierre, Martinique. The crew numbered 47, and there were 21 passengers on board. The chief officer, a man called Ellery Scott, later gave an account of what happened. He saw a great cloud roll over the town, and the sky turned black. The ship lurched, and water rose over the deck. The masts and funnel snapped, and the rigging came down. The ship caught fire, and there were dead bodies everywhere. Ash and water followed, scalding people and covering them in a cementlike coating. Two hours later a French ship rescued the 20 or so survivors.

ELECTRIC STORM

As small particles of ash and stone collide and jostle, they crackle with **static electricity.** Here (*left*), lightning plays around Mount Tolbachik, on Russia's Kamchatka Peninsula.

THE FALLOUT ZONE

When Krakatoa erupted in 1883, its ash floated over a vast area of ocean (above). Some was collected by a ship 1,000 miles (1,600 km) to the west of the explosion.

MOUNT FUGEN, 1991

The smothering cloud of hot gases, ash, and smoke (*above*) is called a pyroclastic flow. Mount Fugen, in the Unzen volcano group in Japan, spewed out lava, ash, and hot gases while molten materials rolled down its slopes at over 90 miles (150 km) per hour. Pyroclastic flow can travel as fast as 150 miles (250 km) per hour.

CLOUDS OF DEATH

During an eruption, clouds of gases such as carbon dioxide and sulfur dioxide escape from the vents. All kinds of materials (known as ejecta) may be hurled high into the air. These can include large, solid blocks made of debris or hardened lava; rounded lava "bombs," still molten inside but with a skin on the outside; and small stones or pebbles called lapilli. The smallest ejecta are particles the size of a pinhead. They make up a fine ash that drifts like a deadly snowfall. Ash may rise high into the Earth's atmosphere and stream around the planet in a long trail.

FLYING INTO THE CLOUD

In 1982, Indonesia experienced a powerful Plinian eruption. The Galunggung Volcano pumped a mushroom cloud of gas and ash high into the air (*above*). Some 75,000 people were evacuated. Whole villages were buried. A British Airways jumbo jet flew into the ash cloud at a height of about 37,000 feet (11,200 m). The dust choked the engines for over 15 minutes, and the aircraft only just managed to land.

Islanders in Montserrat, in the Caribbean, protect themselves with cardboard boxes (right) as ash falls from the sky. They were later issued masks. The Soufriere Hills Volcano began to erupt in 1995. In the following two years there were pyroclastic flows and an ash cloud that climbed 7.5 miles (12 km) into the atmosphere.

DISASTER ZONE

Volcanic forces cannot be tamed by humans. Earthquakes and eruptions can send shock waves through the ocean, piling up massive walls of water called tsunamis. Thousands of people were swept out to sea when Krakatoa erupted in 1883. A major risk comes from lava. Earthen dams and even bombing by aircraft often fail to divert a strong flow. The molten rock can set forests and buildings ablaze. Volcanic gases poison people, and ash suffocates them. As the mountainside shakes and collapses, huge avalanches of rock and snow may be released. Snow or water can mix with volcanic debris to create deadly mudslides called lahars. When Vesuvius erupted in A.D. 79, the port of Herculaneum was buried under some 40 feet (12 m) of boiling mud.

A TIDE OF MUD

When the volcano Nevado del Ruiz erupted in Colombia in 1985, a sea of mud swept through the town of Armero (*above*), killing more than 23,000 people. To prevent similar disasters, countries such as Japan have built dams and barriers.

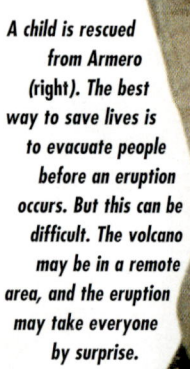

A child is rescued from Armero (right). The best way to save lives is to evacuate people before an eruption occurs. But this can be difficult. The volcano may be in a remote area, and the eruption may take everyone by surprise.

EMERGENCY RESCUE

Everybody must lend a hand during a major disaster (*right*) – local people, medical teams, firefighters, and perhaps the army and air force as well, along with international rescue experts. Road and rail links may be destroyed. Eruptions may continue for a long time.

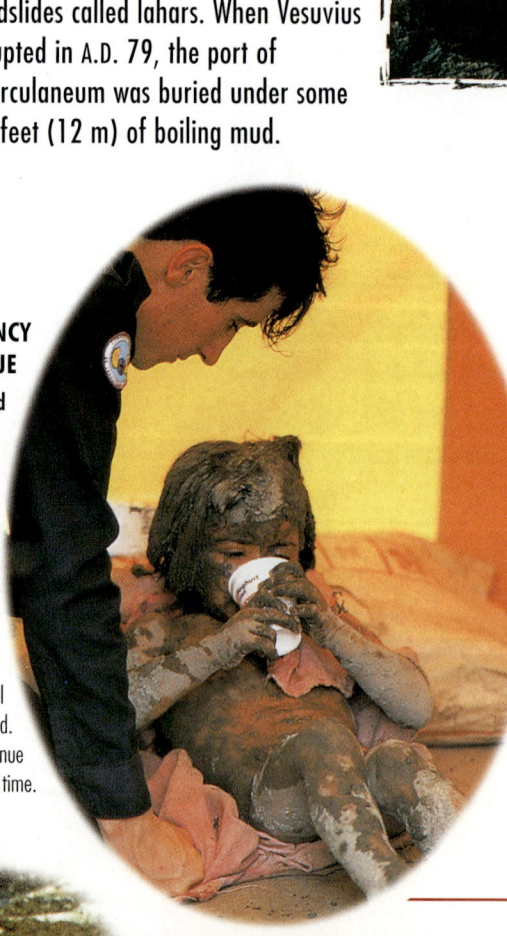

Like a gigantic slag heap, lava creeps over houses on the Icelandic island of Heimaey (above) after a fissure eruption in 1973.

HEALTH HAZARDS

Volcanic fallout can cause breathing problems (*right*), and firefighters may suffer burns.

Earthquakes can rupture water and gas pipes. Water supplies may be poisoned, spreading disease.

Ash from the eruption of Mount Pinatubo in the Philippines in 1991 clings to the branches of trees (above). Volcanic eruptions can paralyze towns and cities, close down stores, and bring transportation to a halt. They often devastate precious forests and destroy crops in the fields, adding the risk of famine to the host of other problems they cause.

ICE AND FIRE

Heimaey is an island off southern Iceland. In 1973 its volcano, Helgafell, was believed to be extinct. But on January 23 a new fissure blew open near the town of Vestmannaeyjar. The islanders were evacuated to the mainland, but 300 volunteers remained. As a new volcano, Eldfell, grew up around the fissure, an enormous lava flow reached the town and threatened to fill the harbor. Many houses were burned or engulfed. For five months the islanders sprayed the lava with seawater, helping to make it cool and solid.

Volcanic soils can be rich and fertile. On the Canary Islands (right), grapevines are planted in funnel-shaped holes. The porous rock traps the dew, and the lava walls provide shelter from the wind.

RABAUL, 1994

Volcanic activity is a creator as well as a destroyer. The Rabaul area in Papua New Guinea (*above*) was heavily damaged by eruptions in 1994. New Britain, the island on which Rabaul lies, was formed as a result of volcanic and mountain-building activity caused by the subduction of one oceanic plate under another.

HEALING THE SCARS

The Mount St. Helens eruption of 1980 reduced whole forests to splintered matchwood (*right*). It emptied lakes and filled them with mud and rubble. It blasted out hundreds of millions of tons of rock and ash. And yet soon after, plants such as wild lupin and fireweed were pushing up through the layers of ash, and animals were returning to the mountain.

WILDLIFE UNDER THREAT

While some animals soon return to the scene of an eruption, others may find that their habitat has completely disappeared. Giant Galapagos tortoises (*left*) had to be relocated when threatened by a lava flow in 1998.

AFTERMATH

The first impression after an eruption is one of total devastation. The hardened lava looks like a landscape on the Moon. Even the mudslides have become as hard as concrete. Peaks have been blown away, and craters have collapsed. Maps of the area need to be redrawn. The release of large amounts of ash into the atmosphere may affect the world's weather for months on end, blocking out the sun. At last, however, life does return to the area. Within 14 years of the Krakatoa eruption in 1883, the fragments that remained as islands had been colonized by no less than 132 species of birds and insects and by 61 different plant species.

RETURN OF THE PLANTS

How does plant life return to an island after the eruption? Some seeds will be carried there by birds or by the wind. This coconut (*above*) has floated in on the waves.

THE VALLEY OF 10,000 SMOKES

In 1912 the Novarupta Volcano in remote Alaska erupted with ten times the force of Mount St. Helens. In its wake it left a new wilderness of ice, rock, and steam. A valley it filled with ash flow came to be called the Valley of 10,000 Smokes (*above*).

Mount Agung on the Indonesian island of Bali erupted in 1964. However, the ancient Hindu temple of Besakih (right), built on its slopes, still attracts pilgrims and tourists.

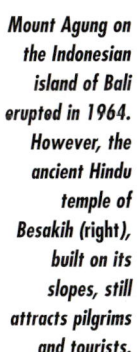

TELLTALE ROCKS

Rocky landscapes give us all kinds of clues about the Earth's crust and how it is formed. Rocks that have been forged by volcanic activity are called igneous ("fiery"). Magma that has seeped up into cracks and slowly cooled forms intrusive rocks such as the very hard granites. Magma that has erupted as lava and then quickly cooled is called extrusive.

CAPPADOCIA, TURKEY

Millions of years ago the Cappadocia region was deluged with volcanic ash, cinders, and basalt. Over the ages, softer parts of the resulting rock were eroded into bizarre pointed columns (below).

THE GIANT'S CAUSEWAY, NORTHERN IRELAND

It used to be said that the legendary Irish hero Finn MacCool built this rocky headland as a road to Scotland. In fact, it is a formation of 40,000 or so symmetrical columns of basalt (*above*). They were created by fissure eruptions about 60 million years ago.

LE PUY, FRANCE

This chapel, at Le Puy in south central France, is built on top of an eroded plug of lava (*left*). It serves as a reminder that many peaceful areas of the world have a violent volcanic history.

RISING ROCKS

Examples of extrusive rock include glassy black obsidian, slabs of basalt, and andesite, named after the volcanoes of the Andes. Volcanic activity brings many precious minerals to the surface. Rich deposits of copper, silver, and gold surround the Pacific Ring of Fire. Diamonds, formed in the mantle, are carried to the surface by rising currents of magma.

Pumice (right) is a rock formed from frothy lava that is full of gas. It may contain so many bubble holes that it is light enough to float on water.

Diamond Head (*right*) is an extinct volcano crater in Honolulu, Hawaii. Once the site of a defense fort, it is now a state monument.

CRATER LAKE, OREGON

Crater Lake (*right*) **lies in the Cascade Range.** It was formed about 6,800 years ago, after Mount Mazama collapsed, creating a vast caldera. This soon filled with rain and melting snow to form a beautiful blue lake. The little island in the lake was made by volcanic activity after the caldera formed.

NGORONGORO CRATER

A giant crack in the Earth's crust runs down eastern Africa. Over millions of years many volcanoes formed on both sides of this Great Rift Valley. One was Ngorongoro, in what is now Tanzania. The volcano eventually collapsed, forming a huge caldera about 12 miles (20 km) across. The rim rises 1,300 to 2,000 feet (400 to 600 m) above the caldera's floor, which provides a grassy haven (*left*) for rhinoceroses, wildebeests, gazelles, lions, and zebras.

LIFE AFTER LAVA

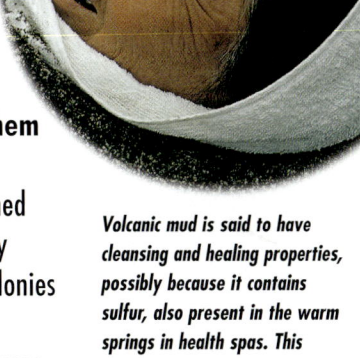

All around the world there are extinct or inactive volcanoes, craters, and calderas. Some of them look extraordinary, but others have become much harder to recognize. Years of erosion may have turned tall peaks into gentle mounds, covered with grass or forest. Craters may have filled with water to become deep lakes. In warm, tropical seas, colonies of little creatures called corals often form chalky structures on the submerged slopes of a volcano. If the inside of the mountain then collapses and sinks down to the ocean floor, these corals will remain in a large ring-shaped reef, forming an atoll.

Volcanic mud is said to have cleansing and healing properties, possibly because it contains sulfur, also present in the warm springs in health spas. This Japanese lady (above) is buried up to her neck as she takes a volcanic mud "bath."

BEACHES OF BLACK SAND

Not all beaches are made up of white or yellow sand. Many tourist destinations have beaches that are black. These include the Greek island of Thíra (*left*), the Caribbean island of Martinique, and the island of Bali in Indonesia. All are volcanic danger zones. Their grains of sand have been worn down from lava flows that have plunged into the sea.

HOW AN ATOLL IS FORMED

FRINGING REEF

A volcano grows from the ocean bed. Corals grow around its slopes.

BARRIER REEF

The volcano collapses and begins to sink.

ATOLL   LAGOON

The volcano vanishes, leaving behind an atoll.

RINGED WITH CORAL

Coral atolls are rings of coral that are scattered across the South Pacific like a string of pearls. They have formed around submarine volcanoes and teem with marine life.

GEOTHERMAL POWER

The heat given out by underground magma can be harnessed to provide energy on the surface (*above*). The heat may be used to turn water into steam, which can drive turbines to generate electricity.

VOLCANO SCIENCE

Volcanology is the scientific study of magma and volcanoes. Volcanologists try to find out how the Earth functions. In doing this, they may help save lives and find new ways in which the destructive power of volcanic activity can be put to good use. Today, some volcanologists can study signals from satellites out in space, which use laser beams to measure the movements of tectonic plates. Others go down in minisubmarines to explore the oceanic crust. Volcanologists may also set off deliberate explosions and record the shock waves that return, in order to find out about the structure of the planet. They may even descend into the terrifying inferno of a volcano's crater.

ON THE BRINK

Volcanologists study active volcanoes and lava flows up close (*right*). They fill jars with gases and take samples of lava, which they can analyze back in the laboratory. They measure temperatures. A normal thermometer would melt, so they use metal probes called thermocouples.

SURVIVAL KIT

While working on the mountain, a volcanologist needs to wear a gas mask (*left*) and protective clothing. Research is often very dangerous, and some samples can be collected only by using special robotic machines.

SOME LIKE IT HOT

Tube worms cluster around a hot vent (*above*), in the Galápagos region of the Pacific. Scientists have used minisubmarines to explore hydrothermal vents at mid-ocean ridges and elsewhere. Heated water rich in minerals wells up from below through these vents. Bacteria-like microorganisms feed on the minerals. These tiny organisms provide food for tube worms and other strange creatures.

THE EARTH'S HEARTBEAT

Seismographs are instruments that are used to measure earthquakes and tremors. The information they provide (*left*) helps scientists estimate the timing and strength of volcanic eruptions. The shock waves increase dramatically just before a major volcanic disaster.

JAPAN, 1952

THE WRONG PLACE AT THE WRONG TIME

On September 17, 1952, the crew of a fishing boat reported an explosion beneath the sea. Their position was about 250 miles (400 km) south of Tokyo, on the Pacific rim. A volcanic island grew up on the spot, but was promptly blown up in a series of eruptions. Japanese volcanologists hurried to the scene. The research vessel Sinyo-maru arrived and began to record the dramatic volcanic activity. Another research ship, the Kaiyo-maru, also sailed to the scene. It sailed right over a vent just as it blew. The crew of 22 and seven volcanologists were killed as the ship was blasted apart.

BURIED IN ASH

In Pompeii the bodies of the victims were destroyed by the hot ash (*right*). However, their shape remained in the ash when it hardened. By filling these hollows with plaster or resin, archaeologists can re-create the bodies as they were at the time of death.

Plaster casts show the tragic, huddled figures of Pompeii's victims (above). They are a moving memorial to all who have suffered from volcanic catastrophe through the ages.

PREHISTORIC FOOTPRINTS

These footprints (*left*) were made by ancestors of human beings walking in soft volcanic ash about 3.6 million years ago. When the ash turned into hard rock, the footprints were preserved. They were found at Laetoli, Tanzania, in 1976.

UNCOVERING THE PAST

One branch of volcano science has been of great use in studying history. When volcanoes cover the land with ash or lava, they often bury and preserve people's bodies, as well as buildings and streets, jewelry, pots and pans, and other evidence of everyday life. Excavating such sites is like opening a time capsule. We find out how people lived long ago. The most famous example is the Italian town of Pompeii, buried by the eruption of Vesuvius in A.D. 79. The site was first uncovered in 1748. Since then we have discovered how Romans ate, shopped, and did business, what their houses were like, and even what plants were grown in their gardens.

This fine dolphin jar (above) was discovered on Thíra.

LONG-LOST PAINTINGS

This wall painting (*right*), uncovered at Akrotíri, on the Greek island of Thíra, shows boys boxing. Other paintings show fashionable ladies, houses, and boats. When Thíra was destroyed by a volcano around 1500 B.C., it was part of the fabulous Minoan civilization of Crete.

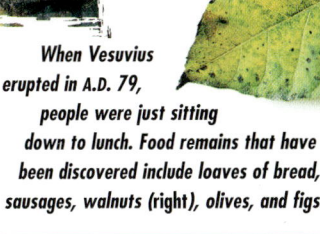

When Vesuvius erupted in A.D. 79, people were just sitting down to lunch. Food remains that have been discovered include loaves of bread, sausages, walnuts (right), olives, and figs.

VOLCANOES IN SPACE

THE MAN IN THE MOON

Earth's Moon (*above*) has dark patterns on its surface that look like a face. The astronomer Galileo Galilei (1564-1642) called them maria (Latin for "seas"). They are, in fact, plains of basaltic lava that oozed out from fissures and rifts about 2–4 billion years ago.

Where is the biggest known volcano? It can be found not on Earth – but on Mars. And if we traveled to Venus, we would find volcanoes rising as high as 3 miles (5 km) or more, hardened flows of lava, and great slabs of basalt. On Io, a moon of Jupiter, ejecta are hurled from volcanoes at speeds of up to 2,000 miles (3,000 km) per hour. Volcano science can help us discover how other planets and moons have formed around our Sun. At some time in the future, humans may leave our Solar System and settle on planets circling other stars. If so, they will have to understand just how those planets were formed and the part played by volcanic gases in the development of their atmospheres.

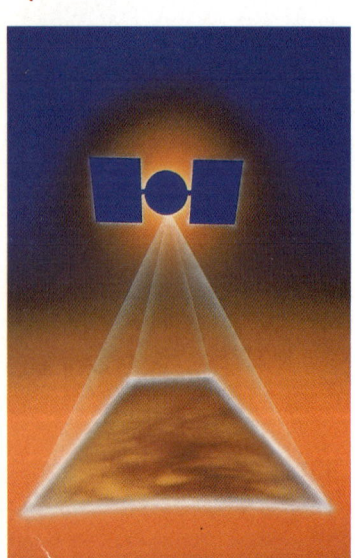

RADAR MAPPING

The *Magellan* space probe mapped the surface of the planet Venus in 1990-92. It used radar signals (*above*) to penetrate the thick, poisonous yellow clouds that surround the planet. Venus may be named after the Roman goddess of love, but the surface of this planet is more like hell. It includes baking deserts, immense volcanoes, massive lava flows, and hot spots where the rising magma makes the planet's surface bulge outward.

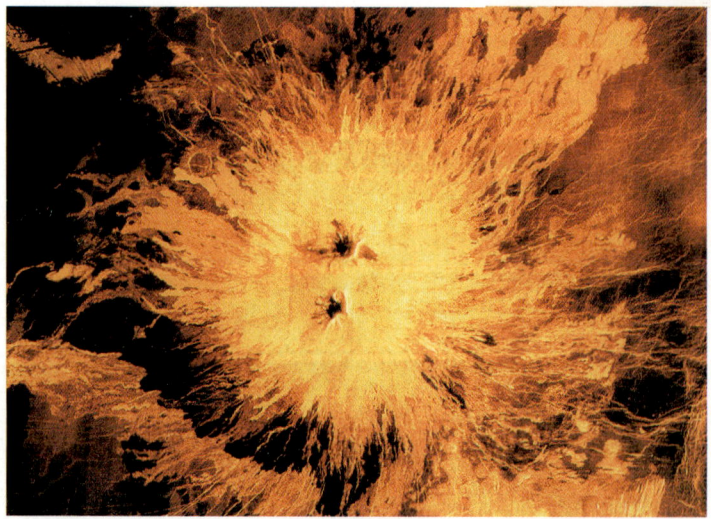

HOT VENUS

Sapas Mons is one of the volcanoes that rise above the plains of Venus. It is about 250 miles (400 km) from side to side and 0.9 mile (1.5 km) high. This aerial view (*above*) is based on a radar image beamed back to Earth from *Magellan*. At the summit are two eroded tables of rock. Around them is new, rough lava (shown here as bright yellow), giving way to older, smoother flows (dark brown, *top left*).

The volcanoes on Mars are probably extinct, but they are still impressive. This atist's view (*below*) focuses on the Martian volcanoes Arsia, Pavonis, and Ascraeus Mons. The biggest volcano known on any planet, Olympus Mons, rises in the distance.

Olympus Mons is a giant volcano, 15 miles (25 km) high – three times the height of Mount Everest, the highest peak on Earth – and a fantastic 370 miles (600 km) across.

JUPITER'S MOON IO

You can't get much more volcanic than Io. The gravity of Jupiter (the biggest planet in the Solar System), combined with that of Io's large sister moons, stretches and pulls at Io's rocks, thus generating heat. Major eruptions happen all the time. Some of them may be hotter than 1,000 °F (500 °C). The moon's surface is covered with ejecta. This picture (*above*) was beamed back to Earth from the space probe *Galileo* in 1995.

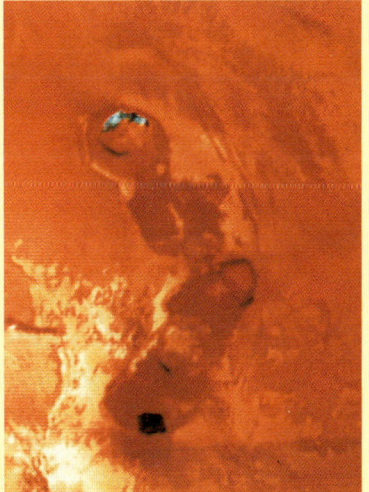

The strange, volcanic world of Io was first glimpsed by the Voyager space probes in the 1970s. This picture (left), sent back from Voyager 1, shows a bluish gas being pumped out from volcanic vents. Since Io's gravity is not very strong, the gases rise to great heights. They probably contain sulfur or sulfur dioxide.

DID YOU KNOW?

The catastrophic eruption of a volcano on the island of Thíra around 1500 B.C. may have given birth to the Greek legends of Atlantis, a civilized land that was lost beneath the ocean waves.

Indonesia, made up of thousands of mountainous islands, is the most volcanic country on Earth. At least 130 of its hundreds of volcanoes are believed to be active.

The highest active volcano, Ojos del Salado in the Andes Mountains on the border between Chile and Argentina, rises 22,595 feet (6,887 m) above sea level.

If you measure height from the volcano's base, however, the tallest active volcano is probably Hawaii's Mauna Loa. Its summit is only 13,680 ft (4,170 m) above sea level but rises some 12 miles (19 km) above the volcano's base in the ocean floor.

The Greek philosopher Empedocles (in around 490-430 B.C.) lived on Sicily. He is said to have wanted to disappear from this world suddenly, so that his supporters would believe he was a god. He therefore jumped into the crater of Mount Etna. But, the volcano threw back one of his sandals, proving that he had died like a mere mortal.

When Mount Pelée erupted on the island of Martinique in 1902, 25-year-old Auguste Ciparis was in jail. He was one of only two people to survive in the city of St. Pierre. The reason? His cell was underground, it had thick walls, and its tiny air vent faced away from the mountain. He later became famous and toured the United States as a circus attraction.

In 1943, residents of the Mexican villages of Paricutín and San Juan Parangaricutiro, about 200 miles (300 km) west of Mexico City, witnessed the birth of a new volcano in their fields. It was named Paricutín. The volcano grew 1,000 feet (300 m) high in the first year and then buried the villages in lava.

In 1986 an invisible cloud of the poisonous gas carbon dioxide rolled out of Nyos, a crater lake in the West African country of Cameroon. The gas, which came from magma below the lake floor, killed more than 1,700 people.

The northernmost active volcano is Beerenberg, on Jan Mayen, a Norwegian island in the Arctic Ocean. The southernmost is the impressive Mount Erebus, which towers over the icy wastes of Antarctica.

GLOSSARY

basalt - a common type of rock formed from magma

core - the ball-shaped central part of the Earth, composed mostly of iron and nickle and lying below the mantle

crust - the thin, solid outer layer of the Earth; it is thinner under the oceans than the continents, where its thickness averages about 25 miles (40 km) and can be as much as 45 miles (70 km) or more in mountainous areas

ejecta - material thrown out from a volcano

fissure - a crack or fracture in rock

fumarole - a vent in a volcanic area that releases gases or fumes

hydrothermal vent - a vent in the ocean floor that releases hot, mineral-rich water from below

lahar - a mudflow down the slope of a volcano created when ash or volcanic debris becomes mixed with water

lava - magma that emerges on the surface of the Earth; the word "lava" is also used to refer to this magma after it cools down and becomes solid

magma - molten rock below the surface of the Earth; magma that appears on the surface is called lava

mantle - the layer within the Earth that lies between the crust and the core; it is about 1,800 miles (2,900 km) thick

mid-ocean ridge - a raised section of the ocean floor running along a rift where two oceanic plates are moving apart

plate - or tectonic plate, one of several rigid pieces that make up the Earth's outer layer; movements of the plates play a role in many earthquakes and the formation of many volcanoes

plug - a pipelike, usually vertical body of magma or lava that came from a volcanic vent; a solidified plug may remain standing if surrounding rock is eroded away

rift - a crack where pieces of the Earth's surface, such as plates, are moving apart

St. Elmo's fire - a light-producing electrical discharge seen during a storm on objects that have a pointed shape or are high up

static electricity - electric charge that builds up in certain materials when they rub against other materials

subduction - the process that occurs when two tectonic plates collide and the edge of one plate descends below the other and enters the mantle

tremor - a small earthquake, especially one preceding or following a major quake

vent - an opening in the Earth's surface through which lava, gases, or other volcanic materials come from below

INDEX